Dedicated to the dreamers.

May you always feel invited.

Library of Congress Cataloging-in-Publication Data
Names: Miyares, Daniel, author, illustrator.
Title: Night out / by Daniel Miyares.
Description: First edition. | New York : Schwartz & Wade Books, [2018] Summary: Newly-arrived at
boarding school, a boy finds an invitation and goes on an adventure that may lead to friendship.
Identifiers: LCCN 2017043015 (print) | LCCN 2017056323 (ebook) | ISBN 978-1-5247-6574-3 (eBook)
ISBN 978-1-5247-6572-9 (hardcover) | ISBN 978-1-5247-6573-6 (library binding)

Subjects: | CYAC: Adventure and adventurers—Fiction. | Friendship—Fiction.
Boarding schools—Fiction. | Schools—Fiction.
Classification: LCC PZ7.M699577 (ebook) | LCC PZ7.M699577 Nig 2018 (print) | DDC [E]—dc23
Visit us on the Web! rhcbooks.com
Educators and librarians, for a variety of teaching tools, visit us at RHTeachersLibrarians.com
The text of this book was hand lettered by the artist.
The illustrations were rendered in gouache and colored
pencils on Strathmore paper.
MANUFACTURED IN CHINA
10 9 8 7 6 5 4 3 2 1
First Edition

NIGHT OUT

by Daniel Miyares

schwartz & wade books   new york

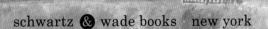

All alone.

An invitation?

A decision.

And a journey begins.

A friend.

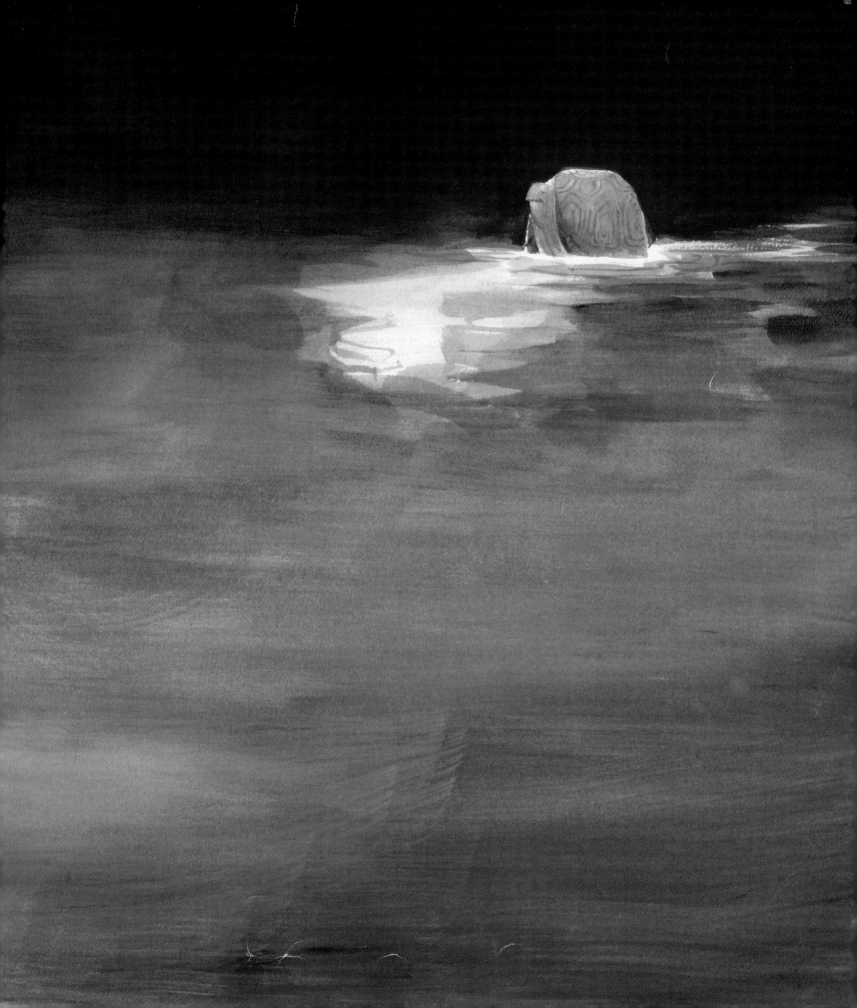

"You're just in time...

...for tea."

"And a song!"

A night out ends,

And a new day begins.

A story to share.